The Goodbye Time

ALSO BY CELESTE CONWAY

The Melting Season

The Goodbye Time

Celeste Conway

Delacorte Press

Published by Delacorte Press
an imprint of Random House Children's Books
a division of Random House, Inc.
New York

Delacorte Press and colophon are registered trademarks of Random House, Inc.

Visit us on the Web! www.randomhouse.com/kids

Educators and librarians, for a variety of teaching tools, visit us at
www.randomhouse.com/teachers

Library of Congress Cataloging-in-Publication Data is available upon request.

ISBN: 978-0-385-73555-1 (trade)
ISBN: 978-0-385-90540-4 (lib bdg.)

The text of this book is set in 12.5-point Goudy.
Book design by Stephanie Moss

Printed in the United States of America

10 9 8 7 6 5 4 3 2 1

First Edition

To Peg and Chris,
the roses around the thorn

The Goodbye Time

Chapter One

Kendra was talking about the dress again. The one she had gotten for fifth-grade graduation which came from France, according to her, and was made of something called white "pee-kay." We'd heard about it at least fifty times. But I guess she needed to tell us again. Then Nancy Palmer started in on *her* dress. The dress she was *going to* get, that is, at some showroom that her mother knew where designers sold their latest stuff.

"Your mom knows designers?" Kendra said, flipping back her smooth black hair.

Nancy nodded. "Lots of them."

"Wow, you're lucky. I bet you can get your dress half price."

That was when my best friend, Katy, gave me a signal with her eyes and I knew we were going to leave them all—all our friends walking down the hall at school on a Friday afternoon in May. We were right at the place where the kindergarten artwork hung—potato prints and fingerpaints—and I looked at Katy and nodded. And just like that, we weren't there. Oh, our bodies were there, still a little sweaty from gym class, but *we* were gone, because now we were being someone else.

We did it almost all the time. We sort of couldn't stop ourselves, though sometimes I think we wanted to. We knew it was weird. Worse than weird—abnormal. And we'd both have just *died* if anyone had known. No one did. People would have worried. Even our families probably would have thought it was unhealthy.

The three o'clock schoolyard bustled with activity as we stepped outside. Nannies and moms were picking up kids, and our friends were going on and on about graduation dresses, but Katy and I were far away. We were in our own world, the one we went into by ourselves, pretending to be our characters. It was our favorite thing to do.

It had only been a few months ago, when I turned eleven, that my parents started letting me walk home from school alone. Up until then this high school girl, Miranda, who lives in my building, would get ten dollars for walking me two blocks from Seventy-eighth Street to

Eightieth Street and another three blocks over to River-side Drive, which is where I live in Manhattan, New York City. And actually, I'm still not allowed to walk home alone; I have to be with Katy.

Katy used to come home with me a lot: She lives up-town, and her apartment wasn't that great back then. I mean, it wasn't terrible, but she has a little brother, Sam, who has something wrong with him called profound intellectual and developmental disability, and he would make a mess, throwing things and sometimes doing certain stuff I wouldn't want to mention here. Also, she had to share a room with her older sister, who she called Bug Eye and who was very mean and was always telling us not to touch anything in her big fairy collection. Like anyone would *want* to fool around with her creepy fairy dolls. Bug Eye only cared about two things in life: fairies and soccer.

When we reached the corner of Broadway, everyone started splitting up. Kendra and Nancy headed south, while Tyesha went north and Yolanda east. Then, at last, Katy and I were by ourselves. As we walked toward my building near Riverside Park, we started to play for real—that's what we called it, playing, talking the way we did in our English accents.

Chapter Two

The one person on this whole planet who would've understood our game and not thought we were crazy was my brother, Tom. Tom was fifteen and was going away to college at the end of the summer. My mom was both happy and sad about this. That was what she said: "I'm so happy and so sad," like a confused person. Tom is gifted in the brain department, but although he's a genius who has skipped a few grades, he's not snobby about how smart he is. Actually, he says it's a burden being brainy, like having a big rock tied to his head.

The reason I say Tom understood the thing Katy and I did is because when he was younger, he had this thing about Franklin Delano Roosevelt. Roosevelt was the thirty-second President of the United States, and Tom was just crazy about the guy. He read everything ever written about FDR's life and about his wife, Eleanor, and sometimes he'd go around pretending to *be* Franklin Delano Roosevelt. On his eighth birthday, when my mom took him to the bakery to pick out his cake, he made the lady write HAPPY BIRTHDAY, FRANKLIN on it. That's how crazy Tom was about him. And that's why I just think he would have gotten it and not made fun of us or told us we were weird.

When we got to my building, the doorman, Larry, said hi and gave me a huge envelope that hadn't fit in our mailbox. It was from Harvard University, the big famous college my brother was going to attend in the fall. They had probably sent some more papers for him to fill out.

When Katy and I first went into my apartment, we thought no one was home. But then we smelled grilled cheese, which was a sure sign that Tom was there.

"Do you think he'll make us some?" Katy asked in her English accent as we dropped our hundred-pound backpacks on the kitchen floor.

"Don't know," I said. "Uncle George is a bit of a lout these days." Uncle George, by the way, wasn't one of our regular characters. But sometimes when we were playing, we had to give other people parts. They, of course, didn't know, like Tom didn't know he was Uncle George as he came into the kitchen quietly in his big white socks. He was carrying a plate that still had half of a grilled cheese sandwich on it.

"Hi, you two," he said to us. He looked like he'd just gotten out of bed, with his rumpled hair and his wrinkled pants and T-shirt.

"Hey, bloke," I said. "Mind making us some sandwiches?" He was used to me calling him things like bloke and mate, so he didn't think anything of it. I knew he didn't feel like making us anything and had probably been trying to sneak back into the kitchen before we got home. But he's a pretty nice guy, and I think he realized how much he was going to miss me when he went away to school.

"All right," he said, "but I'm not serving tea or anything like that."

"Jolly good," I answered. Then Johnny and I (Johnny was Katy's character) started pulling out the teacups and the fancy pot and sugar bowl. I took out my special sugar cubes too, which had tiny flowers painted on them with edible paint and came from some fancy store in England. After that we sat down at the table and watched Uncle George make the sandwiches.

"Don't be telling Uncle Georgie about me bad grades," Johnny said in a voice so low I could hardly hear him.

"I'll think about that," I replied in a stern voice. Then: "If you think you'll be going out on a date this weekend with Clarissa with grades like that, you're blooming daft." At that, Johnny looked like he wanted to yell at me, but instead he bit his lip and lowered his head, really mad but holding it in.

"I'll be putting the water on, then," I said. I got up to fill the teakettle, but Uncle George told me to stay out of his way, that he'd do it, so I went back to the table and rolled my eyes at Johnny.

"Ever since he lost his job down at the fish-and-chips plant, he's been like that."

"Blarky?" suggested Johnny.

"More like wormy." Sometimes we made up words that we thought sounded British, even though we'd never heard any English people use them on TV, which they call the telly.

"You can't keep me from seeing Clarissa," Johnny muttered through his teeth.

"Shall I have a chat with your uncle about that?" I said, all threatening. Johnny shot a hateful glance at Uncle George, but luckily, George was too busy flipping grilled cheese sandwiches onto our plates to notice. They smelled really good and we couldn't wait to taste them, even though it was *American*, not English, cheese dripping out of the Wonder Bread.

"Looks bloody yummy," I said.

"I'm bloody glad," Uncle George answered. Then he turned off the screaming teakettle and ended up making our tea after all. He flipped out his own second or maybe third grilled cheese sandwich, then shuffled out of the kitchen to get back to his beloved computer.

Johnny gazed after him. Then he said, "Doesn't Uncle George have any clothes? I mean, clothes that aren't wrinkled that he could wear into Liverpool?"

"Don't be criticizing your uncle," I snapped. "You don't look so great yourself in those leather pants with those chains hanging off ya and those spikes in your tongue, laddie." Which shut Johnny up for a while. Plus we were busy eating our sandwiches now. Tom could have gotten a scholarship to Harvard just based on what a genius he is at making grilled cheese sandwiches. We washed them down with the tea, which we had actually begun to like.

Chapter Three

By now you've probably figured out who we were when we played. Unless, of course, you don't own a telly and don't watch *Wild Star*, which comes on every Friday night between *Treeville Place* and *Mystic Girls* and is about the life of a struggling English rock star named Johnny. He plays guitar and sings in his band, Riot. My mom says it seems like the life story of the dead Beatle John Lennon, because he was orphaned too and raised by his aunt, whose name also happened to be Mimi, like the aunt on *Wild Star*. But I can tell you, our Johnny doesn't look at all like a dead Beatle. He's gorgeous.

First of all, he's kind of skinny. A little hungry-looking, I mean, like he could use about a week's worth of my brother's grilled cheese. And he looks sort of sad, like a puppy, and hardly ever smiles—so that when he *does* smile, well, it just about makes you keel over, it's so cute. He has longish hair that's all wild but not dirty or knotty. He wears black leather pants all the time, or once in a blue moon, jeans with holes all over them. And he has pierced ears and a pierced eyebrow and tongue, which is the only thing I wish Johnny didn't have. The pierced tongue, I mean. I like the eyebrow, though, because it makes you really notice his eyes. And his eyes, well, wow. They're green with some golden specks swirled into them. And then there's his mouth, which is pink and soft like the mouth of a girl. But the rest of his face is like a boy's, so it makes the mouth very special, sort of like a rose.

I think I know Johnny's face better than any other face on earth. I used to have pictures of him all over my room. Sometimes I'd pretend that the life-sized poster over my bed was the real Johnny. I'd climb on the bed in front of it and pretend we were outside a fish-and-chips joint in Liverpool, where Johnny lives. It would be nighttime, and I'd be an American visiting England. I'd tell him thanks a lot for the dinner, that I'm barmy about fish-and-chips. Then all of a sudden he'd be kissing me (I'd press my mouth against the poster lips) and telling me what a bloody beautiful Yank I was. I did that a lot in my spare time. Once I told Katy that I did it, and she started to do it too. Katy couldn't do stuff like that in her room because Bug Eye was always there, and also there was no space on the walls for a poster of Johnny, what with all the weird little pictures of fairies taped up there.

After our grilled cheese, Johnny and I cleaned up the dishes and went into my room, which we called the parlor when we were playing. We brought our teacups with us, which my mom wasn't wild about, since they're real English bone china, whatever that means. But she sort of liked how we were into what she thought were tea parties, so she let us, even though we might have broken the cups. We were pretty careful. If Tom/Uncle George had ever taken a teacup into his crazy room, it would have been broken in about five seconds.

In the parlor Johnny started moaning about how important Clarissa was to him (that's Johnny's girlfriend on the TV show) and how Aunt Mimi couldn't keep them apart. I told Johnny he was too blooming young to get so serious about a girl. And then I told him it was probably time we had a chat about the Facts of Life.

He looked all embarrassed, like he wanted to die, and muttered, "Crikey, Auntie, leave me be. I know all that stuff." And then I told him to stop saying crikey and get out of the parlor and go to his room to cool off. And Johnny said "Crikey!" again and stormed away to some far corner of my bedroom, where he sulked and kicked

11

the wall and looked all depressed like Johnny on the TV show. On the show this is usually when Johnny's sadness inspires him to take out his guitar and start singing a heartbreaking song, like "It's All Nothing Without You" or "Clarissa the Sky," but since Katy can't sing to save herself, she just pretended to strum a guitar in the saddest way possible.

So I put down my teacup and went over to the door of Johnny's room. Knock, knock. I knocked on the air as if there was an actual door there. For a while he didn't answer: then, finally, he said, "Yo?" That didn't sound too English, but I went in anyway and pretended to perch at the edge of his bed.

"I wish I was a man," I said softly. "A man should really chat with a lad." I don't know why we liked doing this, but Aunt Mimi talked a lot to Johnny about this subject.

"I miss my dad," Johnny said heartbreakingly, on the verge of tears.

"It's okay to cry," I told him. But of course, Johnny cleared his throat and wiped his eyes and didn't cry, even though his father was dead, because that would have been wimpy like a nancy boy. But I knew he was crying inside.

It was like in real life, when the father of this boy in our class, Michael Trefaro, died. This was in January. Michael is really nice and everyone likes him a lot. Our whole class went to the funeral, which was in a Catholic church and was really sad. All the girls were crying, but the boys weren't, except for Matt Harris, who's a nancy boy for sure. Everyone, especially the girls, wanted to see if Michael would cry. But he didn't. He was walking down the aisle of the church with all the sad music playing, with his head down, looking at the floor like all the men, with the women crying and his sisters—his *older* sisters—holding on to him. As if he had become one of them—the men—overnight. After that his mother took the whole family to New Jersey to be near her brother for a couple of months, though they were supposed to come back again so that Michael could graduate with us.

"I know you miss him," I said to Johnny. "Sometimes you remind me a lot of him with your shenanigans. Listen, Johnny, it's important to know the facts of life."

"Knock it off, Auntie," Johnny said, cringing. But I didn't knock it off. For about the hundredth time, I started telling him the facts of life. As if he was a kid in lower school. As if he was *us* in health class, where Mrs. Klein separated us from the boys and talked about menstruation and how it was going to happen any minute now and, in fact, had already happened to certain people—such as Diana Robeson, who's large for her age, and Tyesha and a lot of others, we knew, though not us yet, Katy and me, the two late bloomers of grade five B.

Johnny looked embarrassed, which we somehow

enjoyed, and then I went on to tell him how you make a baby. As if Johnny, a sixteen-year-old rock star with a pierced tongue, didn't know.

"I know all this stuff," moaned Johnny.

"Good," I told him. "And don't be doing any of it. You and Clarissa are way too young."

"Bosh," he said, all miserable.

After a few hours it started to get dark outside. I mean dusky, because it was May and was daylight savings time. Katy and I usually got exhausted from playing around that time, after we'd acted out all the scenes about the facts of life and Johnny's father's death. We just got overdone. Kind of like when you've eaten too many chocolate Easter eggs or a whole shopping bag full of Halloween stuff.

Around six my mom got home from her job at the publishing company where she works designing picture books. She came into my room and found us sitting there looking at catalogs with dresses in them. She noticed the teacups and probably thought we'd been having one of our tea parties and talking about graduation dresses all afternoon, instead of talking about uteruses and sperm and Johnny.

"Hi, girls!" she said, and we said hi in our normal American accents, which aren't really accents, I guess. I mean, not if you're American, which we are. My mom is

14

what they call high energy and is almost always cheerful. Unlike Katy's mom, who is low energy, probably because she's divorced and has no husband to help her and doesn't have an interesting job looking at children's books all day like my mom. Katy's mom works part-time in a hospital but isn't a doctor or a nurse. The rest of the time she was at home with Sam, who is disabled, as I said, and sometimes gets a little wild.

I know it sounds mean, but my mom is prettier than Katy's mom. She looks like one of the ladies in the J. Jill catalog, where she buys some of her clothes. She has blond hair that's cut really even at her shoulders. She's not fat either, like Katy's mom is, and always wears nice clothes and pretty shoes. My mom told me once that Katy's mom has a hard life compared to hers. Maybe that's why she's too tired to worry much about how she looks.

"Find anything nice?" my mom asked us, meaning a graduation dress.

Katy said, "A lot of 'em look like curtains. Maybe we need to go to France."

"Kendra," I said to explain, and my mom nodded because she knows all about Kendra and how she's always bragging about people buying her things from Paris. She slipped out of her work shoes and set them on top of the pile of picture books she was carrying.

"Maybe I can take off a little early on Friday and we

can hit a few stores. How would that be?" she asked. We told her that would be great, and then, as usual, she asked if Katy would like to stay for dinner. And as usual Katy said she would. She ate at our house almost every night. It was a lot nicer than eating at the tiny table in her kitchen with her stressed-out, low-energy mom and weird, mean sister. Not to mention her brother, who didn't really know how to eat and sometimes got mad and threw the food around. I wished Katy could just move in with us, but when I made the suggestion one time, my mom acted sort of shocked and said, "Why, Anna, don't be silly. Katy has a family that loves her very much." Maybe it was true. But her mother was so tired all the time she didn't really say too much to Katy, and her sister was always yelling at her and didn't act like she loved her. I don't know if her brother loved anybody.

Chapter Four

My dad got home, and he and my mom stayed in the kitchen having a glass of wine while the chicken cooked. He wasn't surprised to see Katy there when my mom called us in for dinner.

"Hey, Katydid!" he said to her, as always. I think he really likes her a lot. He kissed us both and we sat down at the table. Then right away he asked us how things had gone at school and if we'd learned anything useful. Katy started telling him about photosynthesis and he acted really interested, as if he'd never heard about it before.

My brother's girlfriend, Anka, had come by and was staying for dinner too. It was quite a crowd at the dining room table for my mom's lemon chicken, roast potatoes and zucchini ribbons, as she calls them. My parents like to feed Anka because she looks as though she never eats. Once I heard my mom say to my father that Anka looked anorexic—that word for people who won't eat because they think they're fat, even though they're so skinny you can see their bones right through their clothes.

Katy and I always stare at Anka because she's so beautiful. You know what Anka looks like? She looks like Johnny, only in girl form. She has the same wild curly hair, though hers is a lot longer than Johnny's, and she has a pierced eyebrow just like Johnny's and a diamond stud in her nose, though, thank goodness, not in her tongue. I don't think my mom could handle that. I don't even think Tom could handle that. She wears black leather too, like Johnny, and this long necklace with a bunch of little skulls hanging from it. The funny thing about Anka is that even though she looks scary and a lot like Johnny, she's really really sweet. She's so polite and nice to everybody, and she has the gentlest voice you've ever heard, like she ought to be singing a lullaby. Also, she's a genius. She and my dad and Tom are always talking about history together. She knows a lot of stuff about the Civil War and the French Revolution and subjects like that.

Anyway, by dinnertime Katy and I were ready to start

playing again. We'd worked out the story details before we went into the dining room, which looks a little English, in fact, with the good china dishes and the candles my parents can't live without. The story was this: Johnny had been into such shenanigans and was having so many rows at high school that Aunt Mimi had arranged for them to have dinner at the Anglican minister's house with him and his wife. Anka was a visiting wayward girl from America, and Tom, well, he was just Uncle George again.

You're probably wondering how Katy and I could do this, how we could be sitting there eating chicken and pan-roasted potatoes and talking (occasionally) to my parents and my brother and Anka and at the same time be Aunt Mimi and Johnny at the minister's house. But we were good at it. We'd been playing for close to two years in all sorts of unlikely places, such as at lunch in school and even at birthday parties with our friends. What we did was we dropped the English accents and just didn't say too much. We let the others do the talking, and somehow it all worked.

For example, when my dad and Tom started yakking about Abraham Lincoln and the Civil War, we just pretended it was the minister and Uncle George talking. And when my mom asked if we'd like more of her famous zucchini ribbons, we pretended she was the minister's wife, Mabel, offering us more vegetables. The only part that didn't make sense was how the wayward girl was so smart about history and knew about something called the Pottawatomie Massacre.

My dad, by the way, is a history professor at Columbia University. He just loves talking to "young people" about things that happened hundreds of years ago, before anyone was born. He and Tom and Anka talked so much at dinner about the past that Katy and I usually ended up feeling a lot less weird about what we did. I mean, what they talked about wasn't really real either, was it? Not anymore, at least.

Anyway, we played through the whole dinner, despite the brainy conversation. My mom served tiramisu for dessert. Katy hadn't even known what that was before eating it at our house, and now it's her favorite. My dad calls her, in addition to Katydid, Tiramisu Kate.

Afterward, Tom and Anka hung out and helped my mom clean up. Tom was just showing off, pretending he did that all the time; Katy and I sure weren't the only ones play-acting around here. Meanwhile, Katy and I went back to my room to continue playing for a while before her mom came to pick her up.

"I hope the minister put some sense into your head," I said in my Aunt Mimi voice.

"Sod all," said Johnny disgustedly, "he's an old windbag."

"Don't be disrespectful, lad. Not about a minister."

"Bosh," said Johnny.

"Do you have homework, young man?" I asked.

"Just some math," he answered.

"Get to it, then," I snapped at him. So then we got out our math books and sat on my bed doing the homework for Mrs. Phillips's class.

"I hate math," Johnny complained. "And what good does it do me anyway? I'm a rock 'n' roll star, not a guy in a bank."

"Pipe down. You won't be making a pound twanging on that guitar of yours." Then we both chuckled, remembering how in real life Johnny is a millionaire and drives a fancy car called a Lotus, which they don't even make in America.

Playing sure made homework go better. It wasn't as boring as just doing your homework all alone in your room. Also, I'm a lot better at math—and every other subject, to tell you the truth—than Katy is, so I could be Aunt Mimi helping Johnny and actually be helping Katy without her feeling weird.

We finished the math problems, and Katy started packing up her stuff so she'd be ready when her mom showed up. Mrs. Paoli never hung out to have a glass of wine or anything, even though my parents always invited her to. She got mad if Katy kept her waiting, because she was always tired and in a hurry to get home to relieve Bug Eye from babysitting Sam.

In the meantime, Tom and Anka passed my room laughing and went into Tom's room, which is right next door to mine. Through the wall we heard Anka's laughs suddenly get all smothered, and Katy said that was because Tom was kissing her.

"Right on the mouth," she added. "Because otherwise you'd still hear her laughing."

"Yuck," I said. Thinking about kissing Johnny on a foggy night in England was a lot different from thinking about my geeky brain brother kissing his gorgeous girlfriend right in the next room.

"Do you think they do more than kiss?" Katy asked me next. "I mean, they're in that room all by themselves. I'm surprised your mom lets them."

"Tom's going to college in a couple of months. He'll be able to do whatever he wants. Maybe it's like practice, leaving him alone."

"Would they do stuff here? With everyone home?"

"I don't know. Don't ask me that."

"I bet they do in the afternoons. Before your mom and dad get home."

"Stop it. I mean it. You're making me sick."

"Why?" she said in this strange soft voice. "Your brother's not disgusting. He's actually sort of cute."

"What the heck are you talking about?" And I grabbed a pillow—the little one with BLESS THIS MESS embroidered across the front of it—and threw it at her head.

"Ouch," she said, not ducking. She was listening hard, trying to hear what was going on behind the wall. It was really weird, and I actually kind of felt relieved when my mom came in to tell us that Mrs. Paoli was there.

As usual, Mrs. Paoli was all ready to leave the minute we came out to the living room.

"Hi, Anna," she said to me in her low, exhausted-sounding voice.

After Katy was gone I took my time getting ready for bed. Even though I sometimes wished she could live with us, it's also kind of nice being alone at the end of the day. I knew I was lucky that I didn't have to sleep in a room with a mean older sister and a zillion fairy dolls or listen to my brain-damaged brother having a fit or banging his head on the floor.

I got into my comfiest pajamas, with the pink and red cats on them, and climbed into bed with my book and a pile of old stuffed animals. I don't play with my animals, of course; I just lean on them as if they're pillows, and sometimes I like to smell their fur.

On the other side of the wall, well, yeah, I did hear Tom and Anka.

They must have been playing a video game, because now and then there were beeping sounds and one of them hollered, "Yes!" Then sometimes I didn't hear anything and I knew, of course, that Katy was right; that they were kissing and whatever. To tell you the truth, it doesn't really gross me out even though I say it does. And I really don't think my brother is yuck. I actually think he's cool. I'm not saying I enjoy thinking about him kissing Anka. Sometimes, though, I do like to think of Anka. I like to imagine how it must feel to be inside her body and get kissed by a boy who likes her a lot, as I know for a fact my brother does.

Chapter Five

Usually Katy and I spent practically the whole weekend together. But the weekend after that dinner, I saw her just on Sunday. That was because all day Saturday my parents were getting ready for their annual Shakespeare party and they needed me to help. This is a big, weird event they do with their friends where everybody brings food and wine and takes turns reading a scene from a Shakespeare play or reciting a poem or something. It's pretty goofy, and I was glad I had Katy there so I could hang out in my room and not have to listen to them, or worse, be forced to read a sonnet.

At first Katy was kind of curious and wanted to hide and secretly watch my parents' friends drink wine and recite stuff. You can be sure Mrs. Paoli never threw a Shakespeare party. Or probably any kind of party, what with Sam running around screaming or ripping his clothes off like he sometimes did. But even Katy got bored after a while. The good part was that there was a lot of fancy party food around, which we could take into the parlor and eat while we played.

The story that day was that I was Clarissa (I played both Aunt Mimi and her) and Johnny and I were at my house, where my dad, who we called the Guv'nor, was having a party with all his old friends from the War. Katy and I weren't sure what war Clarissa's dad had been in, but there was always a war going on, so we figured there was probably one going on when he was young too.

"When is your dad going to finally accept me?" Johnny asked, to get the game rolling.

Clarissa sighed. "When you cut your hair and stop strumming a guitar, I guess."

"I'll never give up me music."

"Oh, Johnny, I don't want you to! Forget about Dad. Someday I know you'll hit it big, and then we can run away."

"D'ya really believe it?"

"Yes. You'll be rich and famous and we'll live in a house in St. John's Wood and drive around in your Lotus."

"And I'll marry you too."

"I'll be Mrs. Johnny Clark."

"And then you'll have my baby." I looked down at my shoes, suddenly all shy. "Ya will, won't you?" Johnny persisted. I don't know why, but it always came back to babies when we were playing these days.

"My dad would kill me if you ever gave me a baby," I whispered.

"I'd never hurt you, luv," said Johnny, and I guess he meant what you do to make a baby, which we both thought could hurt somewhat, based on what we'd read.

And I said, "When you talk like that, Johnny, I don't know how long I can wait." Footsteps clattered in the hall and I whispered, "The Guv'nor," and we shut up and pretended to be doing homework, like Johnny and Clarissa would. But in real life it was my dad, who'd come to say that the singing was about to begin and would we like to join them.

Of course we didn't really want to, but my dad was all excited—his cheeks were even rosy—so we told him we'd be right there.

"What are they singing?" Katy asked in her regular voice.

But I answered like Clarissa: "Some old songs from the War. Poor blokes."

What they actually sing are some goofy songs Shakespeare wrote a few centuries ago. One of my dad's friends, who's also a history professor, plays the mandolin, which is like a guitar, only rounder, and everyone gathers around singing in their not-so-good voices. They all hold photocopies of the words in their hands.

Katy and I sat as far away as possible on a couch. I told her that Professor Willings, who was playing the mandolin, had his leg shot off in the War and that his right leg was made entirely of wood.

"Poor bugger," said Johnny.

And while all my parents' friends sang "With a hey, and a ho, and a hey-nonny-no," we pretended they were singing about grenades and trenches and bursting bombs. In the back of my mind I kept wishing we were old enough to go to the movies without a grown-up. That was where Tom and Anka had escaped to. I'd asked him if Katy and I could come, but he'd said No Way on Earth.

They probably kissed in the movies too, like those people you see who think you don't see them just because it's dark.

Chapter Six

On Monday Katy and I met at our usual place in the schoolyard. She seemed kind of tired, and then I noticed that her hair was a mess, and it almost looked like she'd forgotten to wash her face. If that happened to me, let me tell you, my mom would be sure to point it out before I got to school.

"What's wrong?" I said, a little worried.

She answered in her Johnny voice, "Me nephew went off his trolley last night." I knew right away that she really meant her brother, Sam. "Started flailing round and busting things, and then he knocked Aunt Mimi down."

"Blimey. Is the old girl all right?"

"The neighbors came and someone called an ambulance. She needed stitches, a bunch of them right over her eye."

"Lawd."

"And the daft little bugger. He broke 'is wrist."

"Sam has a broken wrist?"

"Me nephew's name is Jeremy." I looked at her more closely and noticed how red her eyes were. I wondered if she'd slept at all.

"Come on, Johnny. Let's fix your hair."

In the bathroom I got her to wash her face. Then I took out my super knot-busting bionic hairbrush that my mom had recently bought for me. She stood there while I raked her hair and then braided it: I let her use my cherry-flavored lip gloss too, and by the time we were done, she looked pretty good. Not a minute too soon either, because right about then, Kendra and her little clique barged into the bathroom.

"Big news," said Kendra importantly, and before Katy or I could ask "What?" she told us in a breathy voice: "Michael's back. He's going to be in class today." Katy was still sort of out of it, and it took me a few seconds to realize what she meant.

"He's back from New Jersey? How do you know?" I asked her.

"My mom is, like, his mom's best friend. Like, her *only* friend when his dad was sick. Anyway, on Saturday

our moms met up in Fairway and Mrs. Trefaro—
Angela—told my mom what was going on."

"So we got the idea to give him a card," piped up
Nancy Palmer. "A card from the class to welcome him
back."

"*Whoooo* got the idea?" said Kendra.

"We all did," said Nancy.

"But who, like, actually *purchased* it?"

"We're going to pay you," Nancy whined. She
reached into her backpack and pulled out a giant card. It
had a picture of a big calm ocean on it, and above the
ocean were some glowing clouds with golden rays stream-
ing out of them. "Everyone has to sign it," she said, "and
we'll give it to him when he comes in the room."

"Okay," I agreed, and got out a pen so Katy and I
could squeeze our names in under all the other messages.
Everyone had written "I'm sorry" or "So sorry," and it
was hard to think of something original. I ended up just
writing, "Welcome home. We missed you. Anna."

Then it was Kendra's turn to reach into her big pink
backpack. She yanked out two notecards and passed
them to Katy and me.

"That's an invitation to the welcome-back party I'm
throwing for him. It's going to be on Saturday, and my
mom's sister from Paris—the one who bought me my
dress—is making crepes."

"That's pancakes, right?" said Katy.

"*French* pancakes," Kendra replied, and everyone looked at Katy and me like we'd grown up on a potato farm or something.

"Do boys eat crepes?" somebody asked—Jenny Mortimer, I think—and I giggled because it seemed funny. Or maybe I was just feeling strange—laughing in the dark, my dad calls it—thinking about Michael being back and how weird and sad it must be to have your father be dead.

Everything happened the way Kendra had planned it. The girls went to homeroom a little early with our teacher, Mrs. Baumgarten, and then when the boys came in, Michael was with them, which he hadn't been for a month or so. We all clapped when we saw Michael, which seemed a little strange since he hadn't done anything but walk through the door. Then Queen Kendra yanked the card out of Nancy's hand and presented it to him. He looked at the picture on the front, then opened it and read all the "I'm sorry's" and signatures.

He seemed a little embarrassed, as I guess anyone would be with everyone staring at him like that and giving him a big tearjerker ocean card. He kept looking down at the card and I found myself noticing again how long and dark his eyelashes were. My grandmother would say eyelashes like that were wasted on a boy. As if boys weren't allowed to have pretty eyes.

So then, after he glanced over all the messages again,

he looked up and said "Thanks" in this quiet, kind of uncomfortable way. I felt really bad for him, and yet in a way I liked watching him standing there looking like a cocker spaniel puppy. I really had missed having him in our class, and I wished I could make him feel better. I was glad he was back.

In the afternoon during gym Katy got called out of class and sent down to Dr. Pinsher's office. Dr. Pinsher is the school psychologist and is nice and all, but people only get sent there when something really bad or weird has happened in their life. You go into her quiet little office with all the mental health books—I've only been in there once to deliver a message from my teacher—and she makes you talk about what's going on and how you feel about it and stuff. I heard all about it from other kids.

We were out in the schoolyard on account of it being such a great sunny day and were doing what's called free play. That means you do whatever you want as long as it involves moving around and getting all sweaty. Katy and I had been tossing a basketball back and forth, pretending to be Aunt Mimi and Johnny on vacation in the Bahamas, and now that she was gone I was just bouncing the ball, trying to look really active. Bouncing the ball made me think of that game we used to play: "A, my name is Anna. My husband's name is Al. We come from Alabama and"—well, you know the rest.

All of a sudden this voice called out, "Hey, Anna. Pass me the ball." I looked up and Michael was right there. For a second all I could think was: Wow, his dad is dead. How can he stand knowing that? How can he not cry and cry all day long, which I'm sure is what I'd do if my dad was dead? He said again, "Pass the ball," and he was smiling, so I bounced it over to him and he bopped it up and down a few times, fast, like boys do.

"So, how've things been?" he asked when he took a break from bouncing.

"Okay, I guess. I mean, you didn't miss anything." I wanted to say "I missed you," but I'm way too shy for that. Plus, that was what I wrote in my message on the card, so maybe he already knew.

"Where's Katy?" he asked. "You guys are usually together."

"She got sent to Dr. Pinsher's for something."

"Yeah. I've been there. Everybody wants to make sure I'm okay and stuff."

"Are you?" I asked. Then, really quickly, because I hadn't meant to say that, I added, "I'm sorry. You don't have to answer that."

"I wish everybody would stop acting weird around me and go back to being normal."

"I'm sorry," I said.

"And I wish everyone would stop saying 'I'm sorry.' I must hear that, like, a hundred times a day."

"I'm—" If you can believe it, I almost said "I'm sorry" again. "How was New Jersey?" I asked instead.

"It was all right. I like my cousins, and they go to this cool school with a big campus with trees and stuff. It's way different from here, and you take a school bus for about a half hour to get there. It looks like a school you'd see on TV."

"Sounds nice."

"I told you about it in the letter."

"What letter?"

"Oh yeah. I never mailed it." He smiled a little guiltily. "Don't ask me why. I just didn't." He shrugged, then said, "Anyway, my mom's still deciding if we ought to move there."

"For good, you mean?"

"Yeah. She says New York is going to be too expensive by ourselves. And in New Jersey my sisters can all go to public high school because the schools there are so nice. Plus my mom likes being near her brother and stuff."

"Wow," I said. "So you don't really know where you're going to live."

Michael shook his head. "But I'll be here till graduation no matter what."

"And you get to go to Kendra's big crepe party," I said, trying to be funny.

"Yeah. Like, wow. Crepes are just pancakes, aren't they?"

"Not *just* pancakes. *French* pancakes," I told him, and he laughed a little.

"Are you going to be there?"

"Yeah. I love pancakes."

"Good," he said. "So I'll see you there." He bounced the ball back to me. I wasn't expecting it and I also wasn't expecting him to say "I'll see you there" or to tell me about writing a letter to me from New Jersey, even though he never mailed it. So I missed the ball and it went rolling away and banged into the schoolyard fence. And then he just walked away and went back to playing something stupid with the other boys in our class. It was weird. Boy, it was weird. I couldn't wait to tell Katy.

Chapter Seven

I didn't get a chance to ask Katy what had gone on in Dr. Pinsher's office because by the time she got out, we were in science class studying photosynthesis again. It looked like she'd been crying. But of course, everybody who comes out of Dr. Pinsher's office looks like they've been crying. It's like Dr. Pinsher *wants* you to cry. Her whole office is filled with Kleenex boxes. I noticed that the day I brought the note to her.

Anyway, as soon as school ended and I got Katy alone, I asked her what was going on.

She was really quiet when she spoke. I could hardly hear her, with buses and cars driving by on Broadway. "She asked me if I understood how it was with Sam. His 'condition.' She called it his 'condition.' "

"Of course you do. You've been living with him your entire life!"

"That's what I told her. But then she asked if I understood how 'grave' it was and how Sam would never get any better. If I realized that he was *severely* retarded and would be growing into a big, grown-up retard that was still in diapers that my mom couldn't handle."

"She didn't call him a retard!"

"But that's what she meant. Believe me. Then she said that after last night—with my mom getting stitches and Sam breaking his wrist—we had to think of putting Sam in some kind of place. Like some kind of institution where other mental people live."

Katy swallowed so hard I could see a lump bulge in her throat. "It would be for the good of everyone, Dr. Pinsher said. Because Sam's 'condition' is 'taking a toll' on all of us and it's getting worse and actually turning dangerous, and Bug Eye and me and my mom can't go on the way we've been."

"Is that true?" I asked. I didn't really know what to think. I mean, I know it's awful when Sam is wild or doing certain disgusting things, but he can also be really sweet. Sometimes he'll cuddle up on the sofa with his teddy bear and he'll look just like a baby—a huge, hairy baby, but sweet all the same.

"Well, last night was bad. And sometimes he gets a little wild. But nothing like that ever happened before. It was just, you know, an *accident*."

"What does your mom say?" I asked her next.

"That's the weirdest part. My mom never told me anything. The first I heard about the idea was from Dr. Pinsher. Why didn't my mom just talk to me?"

"I don't know," I told her. But what I guessed was that Mrs. Paoli didn't know how to explain it to her, so she got Dr. Pinsher to do it instead. Not that it mattered all that much; it was awful no matter who told who.

"Bloody hell," Katy said, suddenly in her Johnny voice. "I'm not letting them send me nephew off. He doesn't belong in no boarding school." I looked straight ahead down Eightieth Street to the border of trees in Riverside Park. Some of the trees had pink flowers all over them, and they looked so bright on the green of the other trees and grass. I don't know why, but the petals and trees looking so pretty the way they did made everything seem even sadder.

"I can take care of 'im," Johnny said. "I'll spend more time at home."

"Your dad'd be proud of you, lad," I said. And while I was saying that about Johnny's dead dad, I was suddenly thinking of Michael's dad, and for the first time ever, playing felt sort of weird. I mean, sad things that we used to pretend were happening had started to happen in our actual life, and it gave me a scary feeling, like a big hole was opening underneath us and Katy and I—and Bug Eye and Sam and Michael and maybe even everyone— were falling into it.

That night was the first time Katy's mom agreed to come in for a drink. She looked even worse than usual; the huge pink bandage above her eye stretched across her whole forehead. She and my parents went into the living room and stayed there for a long time. Katy and I didn't even try to eavesdrop on them.

"I know what they're saying," Katy said. I figured I knew what Katy's mom was probably saying, but I wasn't so sure about what *my* parents were saying. I got this awful thought about my brother. Like, what if Tom got into some terrible accident or something and got brain-damaged and turned into a person like Sam who was sweet sometimes but also wild and out of control? What if he knocked my mom down and she had to get stitches, and he broke his own wrist doing it? And what if he was never going to get better? Would my parents keep him at home with us? Or would they think it was "taking a toll" on me and put him away in some mental institution, like Katy's mom wanted to do with Sam?

I really wondered about this. It was different with my parents, of course, because there are two of them, and maybe with two people, especially if one's a dad, it would be easier to keep a brain-damaged kid at home. It was awful to think about something like that. Long after Katy and her mom had left, I lay there in bed, clutching my old stuffed elephant, wondering what my parents would do. And not just about Tom. What if something that terrible happened to *me*?

Chapter Eight

The night after Mrs. Paoli had a glass of wine with my parents, I was reading in bed and my mom came into my room to talk. You can always tell when parents have something serious to say. They sort of move differently— slower, more carefully, like they're walking on tiptoe.

My mom sat on the edge of my bed. That's another sure sign it's serious.

"So," she said, "how is everything at school? I hear that Michael Trefaro's back."

"Yeah," I said. I was pretty sure it wasn't Michael she wanted to talk about, even though she likes him a lot and thinks it's a big tragedy that he lost his dad.

"Sweetie," she said, the most major sign that

something bad was coming, "do you know about Katy's brother? Do you know, I mean, that he hurt their mom the other night?"

"Yes," I said, "though I'm sure he didn't mean to. Sometimes he can't help himself. He gets out of control and—"

"Of course he didn't mean to. Sam is very ill."

"Everybody knows that, Mom."

"Anna, what's wrong with Sam won't get any better. In fact, it may get worse. That's because his body will keep growing while his brain will remain the same. He'll grow into a man, but his brain will stay a baby's brain. Already his mother has to shave his face." That was weird to think of. I pictured Sam with a long black beard, curled up in bed with his teddy bear.

"Darla—Katy's mom—has had to make a very hard decision. To put Sam in a hospital."

"She's doing it, then?"

"She has to. It's dangerous to keep him home."

"But nothing ever happened before."

"Maybe not," my mother said. "But the doctors at the hospital said it probably will again. What would happen if he really hurt his mother? I mean seriously injured her. Who would take care of Katy and Gem?" Gem? Who on earth was Gem? Then I remembered: Bug Eye. Bug Eye had a real name, and of all things, it was *Gem*. Like a diamond or a ruby or something.

"Katy doesn't want her to. Katy wants to keep him home, and it isn't right that Mrs. Paoli didn't even talk to her about it. Her mom is mean."

"Anna, sweetie, don't you see? Katy is *why* she's doing it. For Katy and Gem, not for herself. She's terrified that one day Sam will hurt the girls."

"Katy says he won't."

"Her mother can't take a chance like that. How would you feel," my mom went on, "if Katy was badly hurt by Sam?" I didn't think she really expected an answer to that, so I didn't say anything. I'd feel bad, I knew. It had been hard enough seeing her that morning with her hair all a wreck and her face not washed.

"But it isn't fair. It's not Sam's fault!" I felt myself almost starting to cry. It made me think of a girl at school whose parents made her get rid of her dog because it had bitten her little brother, who was poking it with a stick. And the dog was old and had been a good dog for twelve whole years.

"It's true," said my mom, "it isn't fair. A lot of things in life aren't fair. Just look at the television news. You see children starving or living with war. The children didn't cause the war, and yet they have to live with it. Or look around our neighborhood; you see people in wheelchairs, people who are blind or deaf. These are just terrible facts of life."

"But why do they have to happen?"

44

"I wish I knew the answer to that. Maybe it's God's way of making others more like Himself—more compassionate and aware and more creative about finding ways to help the ones who are suffering."

She paused for a moment, then looked at me in a serious way. "Here's where you can play a part."

"What do you mean?"

"I mean here's your chance to really stand with Katy and show what kind of friend you are. One good thing that happens when terrible tragedies occur is that people realize how lucky they are to have good friends." She sounded so grim and serious, it was making me sort of scared. I really didn't know what else I could do to show Katy I was her friend. We had the kind of friendship where we didn't have to say a whole lot of stuff about loving each other. We both just understood that we did.

"Katy needs you, Anna. It's going to be hard for her. She'll need you when she's ready—to listen and just be there. To let her vent and show her sadness any way she needs to." She looked into my eyes and held them. "Do you think you can do that?"

"Yeah. I guess." I said the words, but I wasn't really sure. I mean about what she meant.

The next time my mom spoke, she had switched to her cheerful, optimistic voice. "It's the best decision for everyone. It's been hard, you know, for Katy and Gem. Their mom feels bad that she hasn't had time to give them much attention. Katy's strong—thanks in part to having a best friend like you—but Gem's been having problems." She probably had no friends, I thought, on account of her being so weird and mean. But I didn't mention that to my mom.

"Plus it's not like they'll never see Sam again. They can visit him whenever they want. And people with special training will be there to take care of him—twenty-four hours, night and day."

"So when are they going to take him away?"

"Oh, Anna. No one's going to take him away. They'll take him to the hospital just as if they're going to the doctor—"

"And then they'll just leave him, the way they left Laura's dog!"

"What?"

"Never mind. It just seems so mean to bring him there and let him think that everything is normal, when the truth of it is he's never coming home again!"

It was awful then what happened. My mom's eyes started to fill with tears. I *hate* when she cries, and I wished I hadn't said what I had. I mean, there she was, trying her best to comfort me, and I ended up making *her* sad. She blinked a few times to make the tears go back where they came from. Then she dropped her hand onto my leg and started to stroke my knee.

She said in a really quiet voice, "Katy's lucky to have

a sensitive friend like you." I shrugged. Right then I didn't think Katy was very lucky about anything. My mom went on stroking my knee for a while. Then, after what seemed like a pretty long time, she said, "Are we on for Friday afternoon? Dress shopping, Katy and you? We'll go out to dinner afterward. Anywhere you want."

"Okay," I said, but my voice was flat. To tell you the truth, it didn't excite me all that much. I was too sad and scared for everybody. I mean for *all* of us.

Chapter Nine

On Friday afternoon my mom came breezing into the schoolyard to pick us up. I know it will sound like I'm saying this just because she's my mom, but she looked good. Compared, that is, to the other moms in their jeans and sweatshirts and running pants. She was wearing a navy blue pantsuit and swinging a big black pocketbook, and her blond hair was catching the sun and floating a little in the breeze as she swung over to us and sang out, "Let's shop till we drop!" I was hoping Kendra saw her and heard her say that. And I hoped Michael saw her too and knew what a cool, pretty mom I had.

The first store we hit was Macy's on Thirty-fourth Street. That's the world's biggest department store, and it was loaded with dresses, let me tell you. Katy and I were secretly playing. I was Aunt Mimi taking Clarissa to shop for her high school prom dress. My mom didn't have a clue, because we said the same stuff we would have said if we were ourselves looking at dresses, such as "Hey, this one's nice" or "Wow, talk about ugly!" She thought we were using English accents just to goof around and make the other shoppers think we were visiting from London. She even started to talk in an English accent too.

"Here's a charming frock," she said, holding up a dress that looked like it belonged to Little Bo Peep. We knew she was kidding about the dress. But there were a lot of nice dresses there too. I almost bought one that was white with tiny pink flowers all over it, but they didn't have it in my size. Katy liked one too, but then she looked at the price tag and suddenly didn't seem to want it anymore. After that she started looking at the price tag before she even looked at the dress.

Suddenly my mom said, "This place is overwhelming. Let's zip across the street to Daffy's and see if they have anything. We can always come back here later."

"Righto," said Katy really fast.

So that's what we did. We zipped over to Daffy's, which is on the seventh floor, which you go up to in a glass elevator. It's known for its slogan, "Clothing Bargains for Millionaires." Unfortunately, they didn't have much for millionaires our age. Not in dresses, anyway, though we did buy some really cool T-shirts with a map of the world on them for $8.99. We decided to pay for them and put them on right away. Then my mom, seeming to forget all about going back to Macy's, suggested we start walking downtown toward Loehmann's and T.J. Maxx and Filene's Basement.

It was warm outside, so we didn't need our jackets. It was fun walking along in our cool map-of-the-world T-shirts, just looking in store windows and talking in our English accents. My mom took us to a cafe she goes to sometimes with people who write children's books. It's a neat place with pink tablecloths and real English-looking teacups, and it has a whole long tea menu with teas from places all over the world, like Dakar and Cameroon and Malaysia. You'd think we'd want to keep playing in a tea place like this, but for some reason we stopped for a while. We sat there drinking our sophisticated tea and eating real scones like they eat in England, talking about dresses and fashion, as if we were in high school or something.

"I'd look great in that green one we saw," Katy said, laughing. "Like a walking, talking kiwi."

"And how about the one with the feathers," I said, plopping some raspberry jam on my plate. "I'd look like a parakeet from Pluto."

My mom was laughing too. "How about the one with

the black tulle and the leather bows? I kept thinking of Anka. Poor dear Anka." Up till then I'd never thought about Anka as a "poor dear" anything. And it wasn't what my mom had said but what Katy said next that actually made me feel bad for her.

"What's Anka going to do when Tom goes away to Harvard?" And both of us—my mom and me—just kind of froze. My mom looked at Katy for a second over the rim of her teacup before setting it down, not taking a sip.

"That's so thoughtful of you," she said to Katy softly. "I haven't really thought of that. I've been so focused on myself. On how *I'll* feel when Tom goes off."

"Me either," I confessed. Katy looked a little pleased that my mom had called her thoughtful, but I don't think it went to her head. She was used to being thoughtful, I think. A lot more than I was, that's for sure.

"You know," said my mom, "Anka and Tom probably think things won't change that much. But the truth is, they will. Tom's starting a whole new life."

"But he'll come home to visit," I said.

"Of course," said my mom.

"And Anka, I guess, can visit him," Katy suggested hopefully. "And stay in a hotel, I mean."

"There's lots of holidays," I said. I was starting to feel a little depressed. And to tell the truth, it wasn't for Anka.

"Life means change," my mom said in the tone she

uses with adults. "Change is hard, but that's how we grow."

"But why," said Katy, "do so many changes have to happen at once?"

"I think it's because change causes change," my mom replied. That didn't make any sense to me, but looking across at Katy, I could tell she knew what my mom meant. Sometimes Katy's a hundred times more mature than me.

After our tea we started walking around again. We were heading west on Twenty-fifth Street when we passed a curious-looking store. In the window a mannequin in a long velvet bathrobe was leaning against a fake fireplace. On the mantel of the fireplace were all sorts of statues and odd things—vases and clocks and colored bottles with fancy Arabian-style tops. There was other weird stuff in the window too. Like a leopard-skin chair and a table with legs that looked like some kind of animal horns.

"Let's go in," suggested my mom. Katy and I glanced at each other doubtfully but followed her inside. Once in the store, my mom seemed to move by radar, passing right by the racks of winter coats and big old-lady jackets to a section where lots of dresses hung—dresses for people like Katy and me.

At first it seemed weird and I didn't want to look at them. They were *used*, you know—maybe the girls who wore them were *dead* and their mothers had brought their clothes to Goodwill. That's what it was, in case you haven't already guessed: a Goodwill store. Anyway, we were rummaging through the dresses when all of a sudden Katy caught a glimpse of red material. She pulled on it—and yanked out the most beautiful dress! We stared at it, all three of us. It was really a special dress—cherry-colored, with bows for straps and the widest skirt I've ever seen. The kind of skirt that wasn't all bunchy and gathered in, but more like a great full circle that would swirl straight out if you spun around.

"That's gorgeous, Katy!" my mother exclaimed, and she peeked down the dress to see the label sewn inside. "Neiman Marcus," she announced. "What size are you?"

And Katy said, "Whatever size this dress is." My mom held it up in front of her.

"I think you may be right. It's darling. Let's try it on."

And it really was—both darling and Katy's size. When she came out of the dressing room, which was just a tiny cubicle with a curtain hung in front of it, my mom and I both caught our breath.

"It's beautiful!" The words just popped right out of my mouth. It was twenty times nicer than anything we'd seen all day—nicer than any dress I'd *ever* seen!

"Really?" said Katy.

"Look for yourself." We turned her around to face the mirror on the wall. For a second she seemed shocked.

"Wow," she finally murmured. "Who's the fairest of them all?"

"You, by far," I answered. My mom came up behind her.

"Look at the stitching. Even the little buttons. You simply have to have this dress."

"Yeah," said Katy dreamily. As she twirled around, the skirt swung out exactly as I'd known it would. Then she stopped.

"There's just one thing."

"What is it?" asked my mom.

Katy looked down. "Well, it comes from . . . *here*."

"From here?"

"From a secondhand store. What if, like, Kendra—"

"Kendra? Why would you care what Kendra thinks?" My mom's really nice, but sometimes even she doesn't get things. She tells us stuff—like not to care what people think, or to be ourselves and not follow the crowd. Not that that isn't good advice; it's just not as easy as she thinks.

Now she said in a very firm voice, "Katy, you cannot *not* buy this dress because you're worried about Kendra or anyone else. On the way home we'll drop it at the cleaner's. No one will ever know."

Katy smiled and fluffed the skirt. "Thanks," she said. "I love it."

While Katy was changing, my mom took me back to

the dress racks. She began to search in a very determined, serious way. And suddenly I realized: she was looking for a secondhand Goodwill dress for *me*! I stood a ways back and watched her. She seemed so fierce and businesslike, pushing the hangers along the rack, feeling the skirts, noting how the fabric hung. At some point she turned around. I thought she was going to speak to me, but she didn't. She just narrowed her eyes and looked at me, and I felt my face get hot and red. I got the point. I guess it would have been mean of me to at least not *try* to find a dress, though I'd kind of been counting on something new.

By the time Katy joined us, the cherry red dress over her arm, I was flipping through the clothes rack too. And you know what? We did find a dress. It wasn't as great as Katy's, but it was really nice, much nicer than the boring stuff at Macy's. It was navy blue with bright white trim around it, and my mom said her pearls—her real ones—would look "superb" with it.

On the way home after dinner, we dropped off our dresses at the dry cleaner's. Mrs. Yu, who owns the store, exclaimed how beautiful they were. "Like a dress for a princess!" she said to us.

Katy was spending the night with me. It was Friday, so *Wild Star* was on TV. My parents knew it was our favorite show, so they fixed up the couch in the living room. We stretched ourselves out on the piles of comfy pillows and my mom served us ice cream while we watched. It was a repeat, but we didn't care. We could have watched the same episode forty times and it wouldn't have bothered us.

We were pretty tired by the time we got to bed that night. Katy was curled up on the blow-up mattress next to my bed, and I was dozing off on a pile of soft stuffed animals.

"Aunt Mimi?" she whispered suddenly.

"Johnny?" I thought she had fallen asleep.

"Do you know about me little cousin Jeremy?"

"What about 'im?"

"Did y'know he's going away?"

"Jeremy?"

"Yeah. It's been decided. He's going away to a special school in London."

For a second I didn't answer. Then I said, "That's better for 'im, Johnny."

"You fancy?"

"Yeah. He'll be with other kids like him."

"Yeah, I s'pose."

"And his mum won't be so knackered."

"True enough." Her voice had gotten very soft. "It's just that he might miss us."

"But there'll always be someone there with him." I was trying to remember all the things my mom had said the other night. I don't know why it was so hard.

"But they won't be *us*. They'll all be strangers he

doesn't know. And they won't know how to help him—how sometimes he wants a certain toy. Or sometimes you have to rub his head. I just hate to think of him waking up in the middle of the night and calling for me or Bug Eye, and we won't be there to hear him, so he'll just keep calling louder, but no matter how loud he calls for us, he'll wait and wait and we'll never come." She was crying now. I could hear the bubbles in her voice.

"Oh, Katy, they'll come!" I got out of bed and plopped onto the blow-up mattress next to her. "My mom said there'd be special people always awake to go to him. It's their job to stay awake all night."

"But they aren't us! And Sam's such a baby, even though he's really big." I didn't know what to say to her. I couldn't remember the other good things my mom had listed. I wished she was there to tell Katy all the things she had told me. I didn't know what else to do, so I reached for my oldest teddy bear and pushed him into Katy's arms. She took him and held him really tight.

Then she said, "We're taking him on Thursday. We'll just drop him off. He has no idea."

"My mom says he won't understand. That it's harder for you than it is for him."

"I know my mom feels really bad. But she says it has to happen. She's really afraid for me and Gem."

"You called her Gem."

"What?"

"Your sister. That's the first time you ever called her Gem."

"Bug Eye, I meant. She's moving into Sam's old room with all her stupid fairy stuff. We told our mom—both of us did—that we wanted her to take the room so she won't have to keep sleeping on the couch. But she said she didn't want to. She said she likes the stupid couch and wants Bug Eye to have a room. She wants us both to have a room."

"Wow," I said. "She's really nice. Not many moms would do that, I bet."

"Yeah, I know. She doesn't always seem so nice, but that's because she's stressed and stuff."

"And now just think, she won't have to always feel so stressed."

"Yeah," said Katy softly. "And we won't have to worry that Sam might end up hurting her."

"You can visit Sam too," I told her. "It'll really be a treat for him."

"I can go every day if I want to."

"Yeah."

"It's not like we'll never see him again."

"Heck, no," I said. "And you can bring him Cheerios. And those cookies he likes. And that stringy cheese."

"And his favorite," said Katy. "Gummy worms." She settled back down with my teddy bear and I kind of tucked them in. I climbed up to my own bed.

"I'm glad you're my friend," she whispered.

"And I'm glad you're mine."

"Good night, Anna."

"Night, Katy."

In a couple of minutes she was asleep. I lay there for a while listening to her even breaths, thinking about Sam. I hoped it was true what my mom had said, that he would be okay. Then I started to think of Tom. He'd be leaving too in a couple of months. I knew it wasn't the same as Sam, but I also knew that in a way he would never come back. Oh sure, he'd be here for Thanksgiving and Christmas and maybe even the summer months. But he'd never really live here again the way you do when you're a kid. I knew I was right about all this. If it wasn't the way I thought it was, why would my mom be feeling so bad, missing him the way she did before he was even gone? Which I knew she did, even though she tried to pretend she was feeling fine. It seemed to me that college was a tunnel. Tom would go in and disappear and when he came out the other side, he wouldn't be a kid at all. I didn't want to think about any of it. The tunnel and Tom. And poor big Sam, waking in the night alone.

Chapter Ten

So Thursday came and Katy, her mom and Bug Eye took Sam to the hospital. It had a pretty name, Fern Brook, and was on Staten Island. To get there they hired a car service and put all Sam's stuff in the trunk, but on the way back they took the ferry.

I like to imagine Katy standing on the ferryboat, leaning out over the railing on the deck. Her hair is blowing out behind her and she is looking straight ahead over the blue water. She looks like a girl on the cover of a book. Something bad has happened to the girl, but she is brave, and looking out at the water and sky, all big and blue and shiny, she knows she will be all right. I see this picture again and again. I keep it inside me like grown-ups keep pictures of people in their wallets so they can look at them whenever they want.

What do you wear to a crepe party? I mean, what's the right outfit for eating pancakes, aside from pajamas? I had no idea. On Saturday I figured I'd wait till Katy got to my house and she could help me pick something out. Only thing was, Katy never came. Two o'clock passed, then three o'clock. Finally at four I called her apartment. Mrs. Paoli answered.

"Hi. It's Anna. Is Katy there?"

"We're working on her room."

"You mean moving B—" I had almost said "Bug Eye." Yikes. "You're moving Gem's stuff?"

"Oh, we did that last night. Today we're going to paint the room."

"But what about the—" I stopped for a second. "Do you think I could talk to her?"

"Yes, of course," Mrs. Paoli said. After a minute Katy came on.

"Hi," she said. Like everything was normal.

"Hi," I said. "Why aren't you here?"

"What?"

"You said you were coming over. We were going to Kendra's party from here."

"I guess I forgot."

"*Forgot?*"

"Yeah, I forgot. Don't people forget things sometimes?"

"I guess they do. So when are you coming over?"

"I'm *doing* something, Anna."

"Yeah, I heard. But we had a plan."

"Is that all you can think of—your silly little plans?"

"Katy!"

"What? I mean it. There's bigger things than Kendra's stupid party."

"Like painting your room?"

"Like changing everything in my house. Like what happened this week. As if you care—"

"I do care, Katy! You know I do."

"Maybe you want to, Anna. But you really can't understand."

"About Sam, you mean?"

"Sam and a hundred other things. Your life's so perfect, Anna. Your mom and dad and your great big nice apartment. You don't understand what it's like for me. Having no dad. My mom always being tired. My sister being so depressed that she spends her life wishing she had fairy wings. And by the way"—she paused for a breath—"I get it about the dress."

"What?"

"I understand why your mom took us shopping at Goodwill. And my mom says I don't have to wear that dress. She's taking me back to Macy's and buying me the dress I saw that I really liked. She doesn't care how much it costs. So tell your mom you can keep the dress. *You* wear the dress if you like it so much!"

"Katy!" I cried.

"Goodbye," she said. "Say hi to Kendra. Enjoy the crepes." And just like that, she slammed down the phone. I stood there stunned. Like someone had hit me on the head. I couldn't believe it was Katy saying those things to me!

"What's with you?" my brother said, whisking past on his way to the fridge. I stood there speechless, still holding the phone.

He pulled out a bin of cold cuts, then turned around to look at me.

"Are you all right? You look like your best friend just died."

"It's like she did!" I blurted out. The telephone started beeping and he took it from my hand.

"You and Katy had a fight?"

"I didn't have a fight with her. She had a fight with *me!*"

"Isn't that kind of hard to do? Takes two to tango, like they say."

"I'm telling the truth! I called to find out where she was, and she started yelling all this stuff."

"Where is she?"

"Home. She was supposed to be here at two o'clock.

We were going to hang out and then go to Kendra's party."

"So what happened?"

"I don't know! I asked her why she wasn't here and she said she forgot. Like it didn't matter to her at all. And then she said I only think about stupid things like Kendra's stupid party and she wasn't going to wear the dress from the Goodwill place Mom took us to—"

"Hey, slow down. You're losing me." I took a breath and it caught in my throat as I let it out.

"She said awful things. Like how I don't understand her life because my life's so great and perfect; how I'd never be able to understand, even if I wanted to."

"I'm sure she didn't mean that stuff. She's just upset—wasn't this the week they took Sam to the loony bin?"

"He isn't in a loony bin!"

"The mental hospital, I mean. Didn't they just take him there?"

"Yeah," I said.

"Well, that's probably why she's so upset."

"I'm upset too—I've been trying hard to cheer her up. Why is she being mean to *me*?"

"She's just bummed out and feeling confused. She's really sad, but it's coming out mad. Hasn't that ever happened to you?"

"I don't know," I told him.

"People do it all the time. Think about it, Anna."

"Well, maybe when I was really young. Like if something broke, some really great toy."

"That's the idea."

"And once, the top of my ice cream cone fell off."

"I bet you screamed your head off—and two seconds later started to bawl. Well, that's how Katy probably feels. Only having to put your brother away, well, that's a whole lot bigger than having your ice cream cone go splat. Imagine how mad you would feel about that."

"Yeah, I know. I'd feel like yelling at everyone—except for Katy. I'd never feel like yelling at her."

"I think until it happens to you, you really don't know how you'd feel."

"Now you sound like Katy. Like I don't understand and never will."

"I didn't say that—"

"Well, that's how it sounds. Like Katy's in this other place and I'll never go there 'cause I'm too dumb."

"Look, everything's changed in Katy's life—"

"And Katy won't ever be the same?"

Tom paused for a second. "Maybe not. But it doesn't mean you guys won't go back to being best friends."

"But what if she doesn't want to?"

"Anna, come on. You guys have been friends forever. You just gotta give her a little time."

"But what if a little time goes by and she still wants

to go away from me like you're gonna go away from us? Why do people keep going away?" All of a sudden I realized I was crying. Big dumb tears were dribbling down and I couldn't make them stop.

"You're crazy, Anna. Nobody's going away from you."

"Yes, you are. You know you are!"

"I'm going to college, if that's what you mean. But I'll always be, like, with you. You're my little sister, you crazy nut. You're never getting rid of me."

"I don't even know what's true anymore! Everyone says it's 'best' for Sam to go away, but if it's 'best,' how come everyone's so upset? You tell me you'll be with me, but you won't be with me; you're going away just like Sam, and you won't be living in our house, so how can you say I'm never getting rid of you? No one's making any sense!"

"Anna, come on. It's different with Katy's brother. He can't write to her or call her on the telephone. He can't send her an e-mail every day."

"You'll send me an e-mail every day?"

"Well, maybe not every single day. But you'll hear from me a lot. You'll probably get sick of hearing from me. And I'll be home on holidays and plenty of weekends too." He reached to the counter and grabbed a paper napkin. "Here, you lunatic, blow your nose."

I took the napkin. "It won't be the same."

"Of course not. Nothing ever stays the same. Imagine how boring it would be if it did."

"But why does it have to change right now—and everything all at once?"

"I don't know. I guess it's just the changing time. But what's not gonna change—I mean, way down deep—is us, our family. You and me and Mom and Dad. We're stuck forever with Krazy Glue."

"I hope you're right. That's what I thought about Katy and me."

"You and Katy will be just fine. It's like I said, you have to give her a little time." He messed up my hair to annoy me, I guess, and get my mind away from stuff. "Want a sandwich? I'll fix you one."

"I'm going to Kendra's house for crepes."

"Who are you gonna go with if Katy isn't coming by?"

"I don't know."

"Want me to take you?"

"You serious?" He never took me anywhere.

"Yeah, of course. Just let me eat a sandwich. Go get ready—like comb your hair." He smiled at me and opened the bin of cold cuts, pulling out some ham.

Chapter Eleven

When Tom's away at Harvard, I thought, I'll probably think of this day a lot. How nice it was walking together along Central Park. How warm and soft the air was. And how good he looked, the new green trees behind him, the blue sky shining through the patches between the leaves. I'll think of the way we goofed around, hopping on and off the benches. How we started singing this stupid song—"The ants go marching one by one, the little one stops to suck his thumb"—over and over a million times.

Kendra's apartment is in this big old building at West End Avenue and Ninety-first Street. In the lobby we met Yolanda and Tyesha, who were on their way up. Tom said goodbye and told me to have a great time, and I stood there watching him until he was out the door and around the corner of the building.

"He's really cute," Yolanda said as we rode in the elevator to the top floor.

"He's smart too," I bragged. "He's going to Harvard in the fall."

"Wow," said Tyesha. They were both impressed. Even people who don't know anything about colleges have heard of Harvard University.

When we got to Kendra's apartment the door was open and we could hear kids' voices echoing through the rooms. We went into the huge foyer and then followed the sounds to an even huger living room, where everyone was hanging around. Kendra's mom came over and greeted us, then called out to Kendra, "More guests, *ma chérie!*" That last part is French, in case you don't know. Kendra broke away from a group of kids she was talking to and came to say hello.

"Where's Katy?" she said, looking behind me as if I was hiding Katy.

"She couldn't come," I said.

"Too bad," she said, but it didn't sound like she cared too much. She lowered her voice a little bit. "Michael's here. He was, like, the second person to arrive. Anyway, come on in. Have something to drink. My aunt's just about to serve the first batch of crepes."

I went in and said hi to everybody. The girls were all standing together in one group and the boys were in another group over by the table where the sodas were. It's always like that at parties until someone breaks the ice. Usually it's Katy who gets things going. She goes over to the boys and says something like "Hey, Dylan, your shoe's untied," and he falls for it, of course, and everyone starts laughing and soon we're having fun. But Katy wasn't here, so everybody kept standing in their boy-girl corners.

Then all of a sudden Kendra's mom announced that the crepes were ready. She waved us into the dining room to a table where there were lots of jars and bowls and plates and stuff. Another lady came in—Kendra's famous aunt, of course—with a big tray of pancakes. She was wearing a huge apron with a picture of the Eiffel Tower on it, and was all smiley and cheerful-looking. She set down the tray; then Katy's mom told us to gather around. She demonstrated how to fix a crepe with whatever filling we wanted, then fold it up to eat. There was Nutella and about ten different kinds of jam and sauces and bowls of chopped-up nuts and stuff. There was also a plate of sliced lemons and a sprinkle jar of powdered sugar.

Suddenly no one was shy anymore and everyone jumped right in to take some crepes. It was so crowded around the table that I decided to wait a little while. I knew I wanted one crepe with Nutella and one with lemon and sugar, which Kendra's mom had said was the way real French people like them best. I wandered out of the dining room and back into the living room to get some soda. Kendra's family didn't seem to like furniture much. In the living room there was just a couch and a couple of chairs facing a TV and some big modern paintings on the wall. There was a lot of empty space, only partly covered by a huge, exotic-looking rug. The place was so bare and echoey that the soda pouring into my plastic cup sounded like a waterfall. Or maybe everything just felt weird and wrong not having Katy there with me.

I took my soda and headed toward the window. It had no blinds or curtains, and I bet that at night people looked right inside while Kendra and her parents were watching TV. I took a sip of soda and when I turned back to the room, Michael was standing there alone.

"Hi," he said.

"Hi."

"You can't get near the table in there."

"Yeah, I know. I figured I'd wait."

He nodded. "So where's Katy? I never see you without her."

"She couldn't come."

"She sick?"

"No," I said. "She just couldn't come." He was waiting

for me to say something else. I cleared my throat. "She was painting her room."

"She didn't *want* to come, you mean."

"Yeah, I guess." And then I remembered that Kendra was throwing the party to welcome him back to town. "No, it's not that she didn't want to come. Her mom just wanted her to paint." He was looking at me, unconvinced. Like he didn't believe me. I felt I had to explain. "Do you know about her brother?"

"Kinda, yeah. My mom said he's kind of slow."

"It's worse than just slow. He can hardly do anything for himself. He's like a baby except he's big."

"Wow," said Michael softly.

"And yesterday they put him in some kind of home. No one really wanted to, but things were so bad they had to."

"That's sad."

"I know."

"I can understand how she wouldn't feel like going to a party. I didn't really want to come."

"You didn't?"

"Nah. My mom said I had to 'cause Kendra and everyone meant well and went to so much trouble."

"We're all glad you're back."

"Yeah, thanks. The thing is, we're not really back. We'll be here till graduation, but after that we're moving to New Jersey. My mom just told me yesterday." I tried not to look upset, but the truth is, my stomach dropped right down to my toes. Another person going away! It seemed like it would never stop. "I guess it'll be all right," Michael went on. "My mom's gonna buy a house and stuff. And like I said in that letter I wrote, the school out there is pretty nice." Michael's eyes went to the floor. "That letter I wrote but never mailed."

"Why didn't you?" I asked him.

"I guess I thought you'd think it was weird." Still looking down, he lowered his voice. "And you'd also know I liked you."

What had he said? Was I hearing right? He couldn't have said what I thought he had. But then, very slowly, he raised his eyes, and that's when I knew for sure.

"You're different," he said. "I can't explain. You're not like all the rest of them. And pretty too. And I really like your hair." I wanted to say that I liked him too, but the words just wouldn't come out of my mouth. The only thing I managed to say was "Wow, I wish you'd mailed it. The letter, I mean. It would've been nice."

"Can I write you from New Jersey?" he asked.

"That'd be really great."

"Good," he said, sounding glad. He smiled at me and walked over to stand beside me. We looked out the window for a while, out toward the river beyond the rows of buildings to the purple sky all studded with lights. Then

I felt him look at me. I turned my face and he leaned in close and very softly kissed my cheek.

"Is that okay?" he asked me. I told him it was.

And while I was standing there still in shock, Tyesha, Nancy and another girl came sailing out of the dining room holding their piled-high plates. They looked at us. "You don't have crepes?" As if we were missing an arm or a leg.

"It was just kind of crowded," Michael explained.

"Well, it's okay now," Tyesha said. "The chocolate sauce is the best." There were dribbles of it on her chin. Other kids began to drift in, heading for the drinks. Michael and I went back for some crepes.

Normally I probably would have eaten about five of them, each filled with something different. But right now I could hardly eat. I'd just been *kissed*! I couldn't wait to tell Katy! And then, of course, as soon as the thought came into my head, I remembered that I couldn't tell Katy—Katy wasn't speaking to me. That made me not want to eat at all. But in the end, I had two crepes, one with Nutella and one the French way, with powdered sugar and a lemon squirt. Kids kept coming back for more, and Kendra's aunt—Simone was her name—kept filling up the tray.

Finally, when no one could eat another bite, Kendra asked the girls if we wanted to see her dress from France. It would have been rude to tell her no, especially with her aunt right there, so we all said yes and followed her to her room. It was at the end of a long, narrow hallway with nothing in it, not even a scatter rug. Our shoes made a lot of noise on the floor. Like the other rooms, Kendra's was very large and bare. Her bed looked tiny pressed to the wall and her desk seemed lost, like a little boat on a great big sea.

The dress was hanging on the outside of the closet, as if she kept it there so she could stare at it all day. It was pretty, like Kendra had said, and I don't know why, but it did look sort of special, like it came from somewhere else. Then Kendra's mom said we had to see the shoes as well, and before Kendra could stop her, she'd opened the closet and pulled out a shoe box full of—Barbie dolls.

"Mama!" yelped Kendra, grabbing the box away from her. The Barbies clattered to the floor, and everyone could clearly see they weren't old but extremely new, the very latest Barbie dolls. The shoe box was pink and shiny, and I figured Kendra pretended it was her Barbies' car.

For the moment none of the kids said anything. I saw a few of them look at each other and cover their smiles, but no one dared to laugh out loud, not with Kendra's mom and aunt right there. The grown-ups didn't seem to notice that anything was wrong. Though I knew they'd hear from Kendra the minute we were gone.

Soon we went back outside where the boys were, and

we gave our gift to Michael. It was a big collage of photographs of our class from kindergarten up to now, and in the middle was a sign with the dates on it and the name of our school. It was kind of weird to look at ourselves how we used to be, in our woolen mittens with our bus passes pinned to our big puffy coats or dressed in costumes for Halloween. In every picture where I was, Katy was right next to me, her hair in braids tied with those little plastic balls.

Tyesha's mom offered to drop me home since they'd pass my building on the way. My mom seemed glad when I called to say she didn't have to pick me up. She was hanging out with my dad alone, which didn't happen all that much. As we started to leave, Michael came up behind me.

"I'll see you in school on Monday."

"Yeah. Okay."

"Tell Katy hi. I'm sorry about her brother." I didn't tell him I wouldn't be seeing Katy or even talking to her on the phone.

When I got home my mom and dad were drinking some wine in the living room. They really seemed relaxed. They wanted to know all about the crepe party. I had this weird feeling that they could tell I was different— that I'd been kissed. But of course, that was silly. They'd never imagine a thing like that. They also wanted to know how Katy was doing after yesterday. I told them she hadn't gone to the party because she was painting her new room, but I didn't mention the argument. I felt like if I mentioned it, it would all be real, and I wanted so hard to believe it wasn't.

Chapter Twelve

You can probably guess what happened next. On Monday morning Katy didn't meet me at our usual place. I waited and waited, but she didn't come. I kind of knew she wouldn't, but I stood there waiting anyway. Then, at the very last minute, just before the late bell, I ran to homeroom. Mrs. Baumgarten wasn't there, and I could tell from the noise that something big was going on. Kids were yelling and a lot of them were laughing, though not in a funny ha-ha way. I entered the room and right away saw Kendra in the middle of the crowd. She was sort of squeaking, and her face was as red as the cherry jam we'd put on our crepes. It looked like she'd been crying.

I glanced around and Katy was there, leaning against

the blackboard, not hollering at anyone. Behind her, you could still see the words only partly erased: KENDRA PLAYS WITH BARBIE DOLLS.

My first thought was Wow, what if they knew about Katy and me and our game? They'd probably write it all over school. KATY AND ANNA STILL PLAY HOUSE. I mean, that's what it was, when you think about it, only instead of a regular family, we played—well, you know who we played. It was ten times worse than Barbie dolls; we'd be laughed out of the school. I looked at Katy to see if she was thinking the same thing. She met my eyes, then looked away like she didn't know me. It felt like I'd been slapped.

Then all of a sudden Mrs. Baumgarten marched into the room. The laughter and yelling—everything— stopped, like the noise had been blasting from a radio someone had just snapped off. We froze like statues as Mrs. B ran her eyes over each of us. She let the silence sit awhile. Then, in a voice that was calm but furious, she said, "I've never been so mortified. The fifth-grade class. The class about to graduate. I enter the school and hear you from the office—with all the other teachers there— worse than a kindergarten class." She paused for effect so we all would feel embarrassed. Then, tight-lipped, she said, like we really disgusted her, "Now get to your seats. All of you. And not another sound." We all looked down and shuffled to our desks, feeling like total worms.

Katy sat right in front of me, but even as we moved to our desks, she refused to catch my eye. I sat there looking at the back of her head, which I know so well, with its big fat braid and the little hairs that slip their way out around her neck. It's darkish blond, almost a little silvery, and I couldn't imagine not seeing it there. I wanted to fiddle with the braid, but of course I couldn't do that anymore, and I missed it so much, I wanted to cry. From across the room Michael was looking at me. I wondered if he knew what I was thinking. But probably not. And I didn't think I wanted him to.

Mrs. B made us write a paragraph explaining what happened and then list five things we could have done to "avert" the problem, instead of what we did. She always made us write stuff like that. I, of course, hadn't done *anything*, because I had been standing outside waiting for Katy. I wanted to tap her and ask what exactly had happened, but she hadn't been at the party, so she wouldn't have known about seeing Kendra's Barbie dolls in the shoe box. If she could have told me what she knew and if I could have told her what I knew—well, with both our parts together, the story would have been complete. It really stank not being able to talk to her. And it only got worse as the day went on.

At lunch, for instance, she sat with a bunch of girls she didn't even like. Everyone knew we were having a fight, which made me feel ashamed. In the schoolyard afterward I got up my courage and went over to where she sat reading a book. Other kids were watching, but I walked right over anyway. Let them stare if they want to stare, I thought.

"Katy," I said. She just looked at the book.

"The least you could do is talk to me." She just kept looking down at the page. "That book must be very interesting."

"It is," she said, not moving.

"I'm sorry, Katy. For whatever I did."

"You don't even know. See, that's the problem, Anna."

"Tell me, then. I want to know."

"If I have to *tell* you, what's the point? I mean, how can you be so dumb?"

"And how can you be so *mean*?"

"You're mean *and* dumb," she answered, then slammed the book shut and walked away. I stood there stunned. Everyone was watching, and I felt the tears starting to well in my eyes. I bit my lip as hard as I could to keep them back. Then I sat on the bench that Katy had left. All around, people were laughing and playing games. It seemed like a movie without the sound. I could see their faces, their smiling mouths, but somehow I couldn't hear them. Everything was blurred. Then out of the blur came Michael's voice.

"Hi," he said. He was standing right there in front of

me, though I hadn't seen him until that very second. "That was stupid this morning, wasn't it?" he said with a little shrug.

"I missed it," I said, "but I guess it had to do with the Barbie dolls in Kendra's room."

"Yeah," he said. "It was Nancy who wrote that on the board."

"And she's supposed to be Kendra's friend."

"The whole thing's stupid anyway. Who cares if she plays with Barbie dolls? Sometimes I play with my Matchbox cars."

"You do?"

"Yeah, sure. And I wouldn't care if anyone knew. I roll 'em around and pretend I'm a tiny guy driving them through my room."

"Really?"

"Yeah. Are you going to write it on the board? 'Michael plays with Matchbox cars'?" I laughed at that, and then he said, "I bet everybody in our class plays with toys—I mean, once in a while, I bet they do."

"Yeah," I said, "I still have my stuffed animals. I don't play with them exactly, but I still want to keep them, that's for sure. And sometimes I guess I talk to them."

"Nothing wrong with that," he said. Then, in a more serious voice: "What's up with you and Katy? I saw you trying to talk to her."

"I wish I knew." I was too embarrassed to tell him more. Like the fact that she'd called me dumb and mean.

"Did you have a fight or something?"

"Like I said to my brother the other day, she's the one that's fighting with *me*. I don't know what I did to her. And now she's mad *because* I don't know what I did."

"She's probably upset about bringing her brother to that place."

"Yeah, I know. It upsets me too. But I didn't make it happen. I feel terrible for everyone."

Michael sat down beside me. "I was like that too with a lot of my friends—like Katy, I mean. After my father, you know, died. I didn't want to see anyone. I don't know . . . it just made it worse, everyone trying to comfort me. I told my friends to just get lost."

"Did you call them dumb and stupid too?"

"Yeah, I did. I told Billy Tisch to take a hike. I told him he was an idiot, all happy and laughing all the time."

"That's what Katy thinks about me. That my life is so great that I couldn't understand *her* life even if I wanted to—which she doesn't think I do."

"When bad things happen, everyone says stuff like that."

"How did you and your friends make up?"

Michael looked down at the toes of his dirty sneakers. "I don't know. It just sort of happened naturally. I went away and time went by, and when I came back everything was better. I guess it just takes time."

"Yeah, I guess," I told him. That was the same thing Tom had said. But I didn't want to wait. Katy wasn't going to New Jersey. I'd be seeing her in school every day, and seeing the back of her head and her braid hanging down and wanting to touch it, and I couldn't wait for time to pass. I needed her to be my friend—right away. Like *now*.

Chapter Thirteen

Two nights later my mom came home with our graduation dresses. All pressed and clean, sealed in the plastic dry cleaner bags, they looked brand-new and special. She hung them up on the outside of my closet the way Kendra's mom had hung her big fancy dress from France. And in her cheery, high-energy voice she said, "They both look lovely. Yours is really sweet, you know."

"Great," I said, the way you talk when you're totally bored. I was doing my homework on my bed, surrounded by my animals.

"What's wrong?" she said.

"Nothing."

"Come on, Anna. Tell me." She pushed my legs over, making room for herself at the edge of my bed.

"Nothing's wrong. Except Katy doesn't want the dress."

"Doesn't want it?"

"No. She told me so on Saturday."

"But you didn't see her on Saturday."

"When I called to find out why she wasn't here, she told me she didn't want it. She said her mom was taking her to Macy's to buy the most expensive one." I stopped talking then, because my voice sounded weird and cracky and I didn't feel like crying again. My mom reached out and touched my hair.

"Have you spoken to Katy since Saturday?"

I swallowed hard. "She doesn't want to talk to me."

"You mean not at all?"

"She told me I was stupid and don't understand what her life is like. She thinks my life's so perfect, but she never thinks that *my* brother's also going away, and yes, I know, it isn't the same, but he won't be here like he used to be and no one can say he will!" It was hopeless trying not to cry, and I guess I just gave into it. It was going to happen anyway. My mom slid closer and took me in her arms. I let her do it. I needed someone to hold me awhile.

For a couple of minutes she didn't talk, except for saying "Poor little Katy" against my hair. Her mouth felt warm and I kind of wished she'd keep it there. But after a while she pulled away. She reached for a tissue from the box on the table next to my bed and started to dab my tears.

"Katy's not angry at you," she said. "She's angry at life. At the terrible things that happen. That her brother is ill. That her family can't take care of him. That they had to put him in a home."

"But why is she taking it out on me?"

My mom seemed to think this over. Then she said, "Maybe she's taking things out on you because she knows she can. She has to lash out at someone, and she's chosen you because she knows you'll forgive her in the end. She trusts you with her anger, knowing that you'll still be her friend."

I looked at my mom. What she'd said didn't make much sense to me. How could Katy know I'd always be her friend if I wasn't all that sure myself? Why couldn't she yell at Kendra or someone she didn't like as well?

"Katy's very confused right now. Her emotions are all mixed up. When someone seems angry, Anna, it's usually because underneath it all, she's hurt. You have to let Katy feel what she feels. In a little while, she'll come back."

"But what if she doesn't?"

"Oh, Anna, she will. I promise. And you have to be there waiting, even though she's hurt you."

"It stinks," I said. "Everything stinks."

"Things are difficult," said my mom, "but the truth of it is they made the right decision. Things will be better for everyone. Sam will be safe and so will the girls. Katy's mom will have more time to spend with them. You'll see, Anna. It'll be fine."

I wiped my face with my sleeve. "One good thing for sure is that now Bug Eye sleeps in another room with all her creepy fairy stuff. And Katy can have a room of her own."

"They'll probably get along better now. Katy might even stop calling her sister Bug Eye." My mom passed me a tissue so I wouldn't keep using my sleeve.

"Things will work out. I know they will. Just be patient. Give it time." She smiled at me. "By the way, your brother isn't going away from you. He'll always be part of—"

"Yeah, I know. He told me."

"He told you?"

"Yeah. That I'm never getting rid of him. That he'll always keep on bugging me, no matter where he lives."

"He told you that?" I nodded. And my mom's whole face got funny. Now *she* was the one about to cry. She reached for a tissue and then got up. "Go wash your face. We're having Chinese for dinner. I'm not in the mood to cook."

Chapter Fourteen

Well, things didn't happen the way my mom had predicted. I mean, Katy didn't come out of her mood. No matter how patient I tried to be, she still refused to talk to me. And I guess she went back to Macy's with her mom, because she never came to pick up her dress, even when graduation was only two days off.

Life without Katy wasn't much fun. I started hanging around with Tyesha and Yolanda. They were nice enough, but all we ever did was watch TV and look at pictures in Yolanda's sister's *Seventeen* magazine. Oh, and talk about their periods. They didn't seem to care that I hadn't had one yet and felt a little left out. They just kept complaining about their cramps and their headaches and how they felt like crying all the time. That much, at least, I had in common with them: the part about wanting to cry all the time. The thing about their complaining was that it really seemed more like bragging. Like they were so big and mature now. They liked to talk about Kendra too and how she wasn't so high and mighty now that the whole world knew she still played with Barbie dolls. Yolanda said she probably had a whole other bunch of shoe boxes in her closet filled with My Little Ponies.

Even though I hadn't gotten my period yet, they thought I was cool because Michael Trefaro had kissed me. I'm not all that proud about telling them, but I needed something to make me less of a little kid. And the kiss really worked. They kept asking me all about it. Like what it was like and if I had felt his teeth on my face or any drops of spit. I must have described it a hundred times.

The weird part was that Katy didn't start hanging around with other girls. She was friendly to people, but she didn't do things after school. She just went home right away to hang out in her new and private room, I guess.

In my own room I put my dress in the closet but left Katy's red one hanging on the door. Sometimes at night while I was lying in bed, I'd look at it and pretend Katy was inside it, sort of floating in the air. I'd imagine her arms and legs dangling out. And then I'd picture her head sitting on top. And she'd be talking to me about Bug Eye or about her new room. Sometimes I'd imagine her telling me about visiting Sam at Fern Brook. She'd describe the place and tell me how he was doing. How excited he'd been about the gummy worms they'd brought him, or some new pajamas or the snack-sized boxes of Cheerios. In all my imaginings things were going really well with Sam, and Katy was smiling and her blond hair with the silvery parts was blowing in the breeze.

On the night before graduation my parents made a special dinner for me. Anka came, and my mom made a fancy rack of lamb with those little paper booties on it. My dad popped open some champagne and everyone got to have some, including me. Then he made a toast about New Beginnings, and everyone knew it was also about Tom. I was starting middle school, but he'd be starting college soon.

Looking across at Anka, I had the feeling that she was thinking more about New Endings than New Beginnings. And I guess I was too, now that graduation was the next day and Katy was gone and Michael was leaving the following week. Why do people say New Beginnings when they really mean the opposite? I don't know. But I think they ought to stop. My mom's dinner was really good, but thinking about the stuff I was thinking about made it, well, a little less good. Every time I swallowed, it hurt.

After dinner all of us helped clear the table; then my mom sent us back to the dining room so she could fix dessert. Anka, Tom and my dad were talking about some ancient war where the Roman troops used elephants. I was sitting there feeling sorry for the elephants who had to fight a war they didn't start or have anything to do with when the doorman called on the intercom in the kitchen. My mom picked it up. We could hear her talking for a while in this muffled way, and then she came out to the dining room. She looked at me.

"Katy's here to pick up her dress."

Everyone was quiet. Then Tom sprang up. "I'll get her a chair."

"I'll put out a plate," said Anka.

And my dad said, "I've missed having Katydid around."

My mom spoke in a quiet, very serious voice. "All of you, stop. I know you're glad to see her, but don't make a great big fuss. In fact, I bet Anna wants to just take Katy straight to her room and give her the dress."

I looked at my mom. "That's probably best. She might feel weird." So everybody calmed down and I left the dining room and closed the doors behind me. My heart was really pounding. It was like it had jumped straight up from my chest and was sitting in my throat. I heard the elevator door and Katy's feet on the tiles in the hallway. I took a deep breath and opened the door.

She looked really small standing there in her little skirt and T-shirt with two long braids hanging down in front of her.

"Hi," I said.

"Hi," she said. We were practically whispering, but it seemed like we were yelling in the empty, echoey hall.

"Come on in," I told her, opening the door.

"Is your family all here?" she asked me. I could tell she felt uncomfortable.

"They're in the dining room," I said. "I shut the doors, don't worry." She glanced around, avoiding my eyes.

"Like I said, I came for my dress. Gem is waiting for me downstairs."

"Sure, okay. Let's get it." She followed me through the living room and down the hall to my room. Once inside I said to her, "There it is. It came out nice." She looked at it but didn't touch it or anything.

"I lied about the Macy's dress. My mom can't afford an expensive dress. Especially now with Sam away. The hospital's expensive, and she has to pay for part of it."

"How's he doing?"

"He's okay. I mean, most of the time he seems okay. But some days he cries when we have to leave."

"That's really sad."

"I know. But the nurses tell us he doesn't cry for long. He forgets about us pretty fast."

"That's good, I guess."

"It's really good. And by the way, my mom was really grateful—that your mom helped find the dress, I mean. She wasn't insulted like I said."

"You didn't say that."

"I sort of did. Anyway, it wasn't true." I probably should have figured that out. I mean, Katy's mom is more than nice. I remember kind of thinking that when she gave Sam's room to Bug Eye instead of keeping it for herself.

"It's okay. It's not your fault."

"Or your fault either," Katy said.

"Maybe it isn't anyone's fault."

She smiled at me. "Anyway, the dress looks really beautiful. I bet it's nicer than Kendra's dress." Both of us turned to look at it.

"Remember the day we bought it?" she said. "You were Aunt Mimi and I was Clarissa shopping for a prom dress."

I smiled. "Yeah. We were talking with our accents and my mom started talking that way too."

Katy laughed. "She had no idea what was going on."

"It was funny," I said. "And the people in Macy's thought we were from England."

"I missed you a lot," Katy whispered suddenly. "I'm sorry I was so mean to you."

"It's okay," I told her.

"No, it's not. And it isn't true that you couldn't understand things. You understand a lot."

"But I didn't realize how big it was—Sam going away to Fern Brook—till I thought about Tom going away to college. And it isn't even the same with Tom. We can write and talk and send each other e-mail."

"But still and all, he's going away. He isn't going to live at home."

For a second we were quiet; then I said, "So you want to be friends with me again?"

"I always wanted that," she said. "I can't explain why I did what I did." She kept looking at me, not moving her eyes. Then she said in a very soft voice: "There's just one thing—I can't play anymore. I don't know why, but I know I can't." I let the words sink in.

"It's okay. I don't think I can either."

"Really, Anna?"

"Yeah. It's like something happened inside of me. Or maybe it's a lot of things. Sam and you. Graduation. Michael's father's dying. My brother going away to school."

"Everything's changing, isn't it?"

"Everything but us. I mean us as friends. Promise that won't ever change."

"I promise," said Katy. "Cross my heart." At the same exact second, both of us moved and tumbled into each other's arms. It happened so fast that we bumped our heads together, and it hurt so much we started to laugh, and we laughed so much we started to cry—and Katy and I were friends again.

It's August now, and middle school begins in a week. Michael Trefaro moved to New Jersey right after graduation. He wrote me a letter and I wrote back to his new house on Willow Avenue. But after that he never wrote back.

When Katy and I made up, I told her, of course, about the kiss.

"Wow," she said. "So what was it like?" The way Katy asked me was different from the way Yolanda and Tyesha asked. I mean, it wasn't like she was asking for herself—so she could imagine herself getting kissed—but like she really wanted to know how it was for *me*. How *I* felt and if *I* liked it and would ever want to do it again. Then she said it was weird to think of me doing something she hadn't done yet, but she was happy for me anyway. I told her I would feel the same. I mean, if something happened to her that hadn't happened to me. And then we decided that we won't get our periods until it's time for both of us to get them. That we'll get them on the very same day. We made a pact, the Period Pact. We told ourselves if we really put our minds to it, we can make it happen, we really can.

Graduation was fun, and we had a party afterward in Kendra's big apartment. She made sure we all went to her room and didn't see any Barbie dolls, even in the closet, which she'd left wide open so everyone could look inside.

Two weeks ago Tom went off to Harvard. We drove him there and stayed for the weekend doing stuff in Boston. Then on Sunday we left him in front of the big tall gates. Waving goodbye, seeing him there squinting in the sunlight like someone in a photograph, I could only imagine how Katy must feel every time she leaves Sam at Fern Brook and goes away for another week.

Katy and I, of course, will be going to Central West Side Middle School, where we will be in a lot of the same classes. We see each other every day, and she still has dinner at my house a few times a week. Sometimes now I stay over at her house too. Her room is cool. She painted it red, and there's not a fairy doll in sight. As a matter of fact, when Bug Eye moved to the other room, she got rid of all her fairy stuff. Now she's just into soccer, and the pictures hanging on her walls are of her and her teammates running around or holding up their silver trophies.

Once in a while I go with them to visit Sam. We take the ferry, and sometimes we bring sandwiches. It's a little sad, but honestly, he seems okay. He's thrilled when we bring him candy, and I found out they make gummy everything—not just worms, but all kinds of insects and even mice. Katy's mom seems happier too. Sometimes on the ferry ride, I look at her face, her cheeks all rosy in the wind, and I see how pretty and young she is.

Katy and I are better friends than ever. I think I finally get it now, my father's New Beginnings thing. What he meant was that to have a new beginning, something has to end. Which is just what happened with Katy and me.

Sometimes we talk about what's ahead. How after middle school we'll go to the same high school and after that to the same college. If we ever get married, it will be to guys who are best friends like us, and we'll live in the same building and have parties on the roof and take trips together. And if we ever have kids, we'll wheel them around together like the moms we see on Broadway with their strollers. And our kids, of course, will grow up together and be best friends like us. It's fun to think about stuff like that.

Sometimes, though, I have to admit, I miss the way we used to play. Me being Aunt Mimi and Katy being Johnny. And sometimes—it's strange—once in a while I just miss *us*, Katy and Anna, those girls who played and are gone now.

About the Author

Celeste Conway is a writer, an artist, and the author of *Where Is Papa Now?*, a picture book, and *The Melting Season*, a novel for teens available from Delacorte Press. She lives in New York City.